This book is dedicated to all the neighbors on St. Johns Place and in loving memory of Ms. Denise, who was the unofficial mayor of our block.

Thank You, Neighbor!

Copyright © 2021 by Ruth Chan

All rights reserved. Manufactured in Italy.

No part of this book may be used or reproduced in any manner whatsoever without written permission except in the case of brief quotations embodied in critical articles and reviews. For information address HarperCollins Children's Books, a division of HarperCollins Publishers, 195 Broadway, New York, NY 10007.
www.harpercollinschildrens.com

Library of Congress Control Number: 2020950996
ISBN 978-0-06-290953-4

The artist used acrylic, gouache, and charcoal pencils to create the digital illustrations for this book.
Typography by Chelsea C. Donaldson

21 22 23 24 25 RTLO 10 9 8 7 6 5 4 3 2 1

First Edition

THANK YOU, NEIGHBOR!

Ruth Chan

HARPER
An Imprint of HarperCollinsPublishers

Every day, we go for a walk.

Outside, we see all the neighbors we know.

Even when the neighborhood is crowded
and everyone is hurrying,

we take our time.

On our walks, we stop to admire
the new things we see—

and stick around to enjoy a friendly chat.

Our neighbors keep us safe

and help tidy our neighborhood.

Some neighbors get extra thank-yous too.

Young and old,
big and small,

we take care of each other.

Even when we are worried

or we're going too fast,

it's important to remember to slow down.

And always say,

Thank you, neighbor!

Everybody can get too busy sometimes.

But these words work even in the busiest times.

Whether giving or taking,

or coming or going,

we are a big family.

And that's what makes our neighborhood

feel like home.

Author's Note

When I first moved to my neighborhood in Brooklyn, I didn't know anyone and I felt pretty lonely. Luckily, I had my dog, Feta. Feta liked to go for long walks and I started to get to know my neighborhood that way. I began to notice things I normally wouldn't, and strangers became people I recognized.

Then one day, Gregory said "hello" to Feta and me as he fed the birds. And Margiann said "thank you" as I admired her colorful garden. Soon I came to not only know my neighbors but appreciate them as well. They were doing all sorts of things—both big and small—that helped make our neighborhood a better, more beautiful place.

My neighbors aren't just the people living around me. They are also those who work in my neighborhood—the sanitation workers, firefighters, and construction workers. They're the home health aides, delivery drivers, and bus drivers. They're Mohammed at the grocery store, Tommy delivering our mail, and Herbert sweeping the sidewalks clean.

The more walks Feta and I took and the more stories I heard, the more I felt like I belonged. And when the pandemic hit, I saw all these neighbors—residents and essential workers alike—help each other out more than ever, even when it meant putting themselves at risk. I wanted to make this book about my neighbors as a way of saying "thank you" to them for all they've done for our neighborhood and for helping me call this neighborhood home.

The next time you're on a walk, what do you notice? Who do you say "hello" to, and who might you say "thank you" to?

Ruth

Gregory →

← That's me!

← Margiann